This Book Belongs To

Credits

Design: Anton Gustilo (antongustilo com)

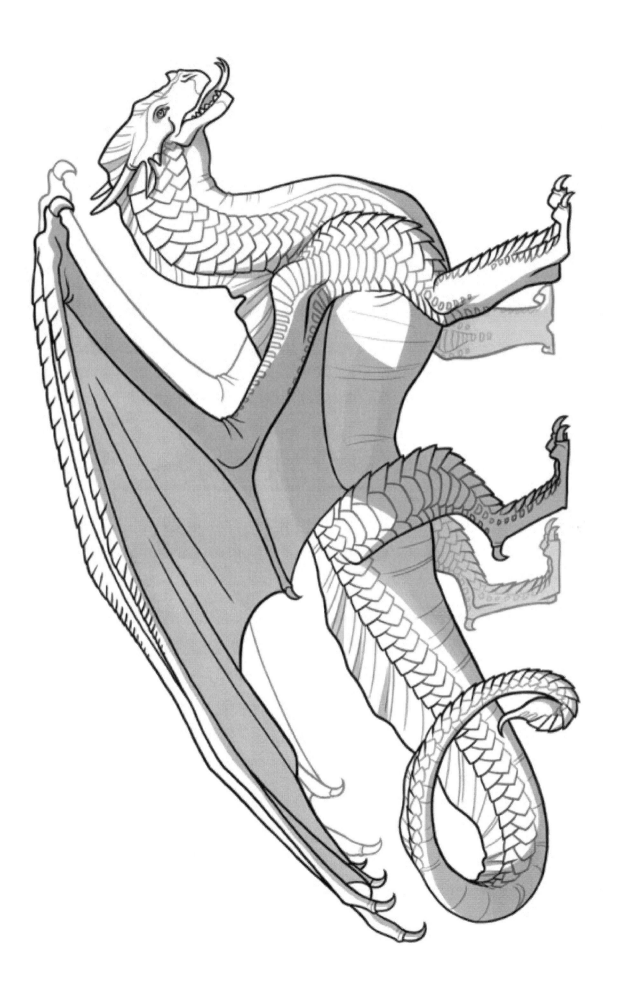

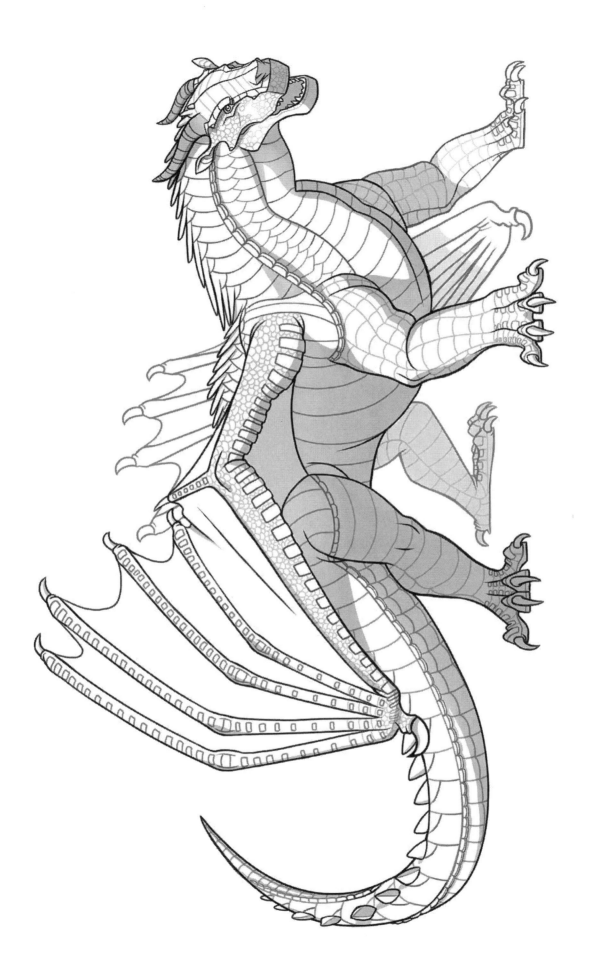

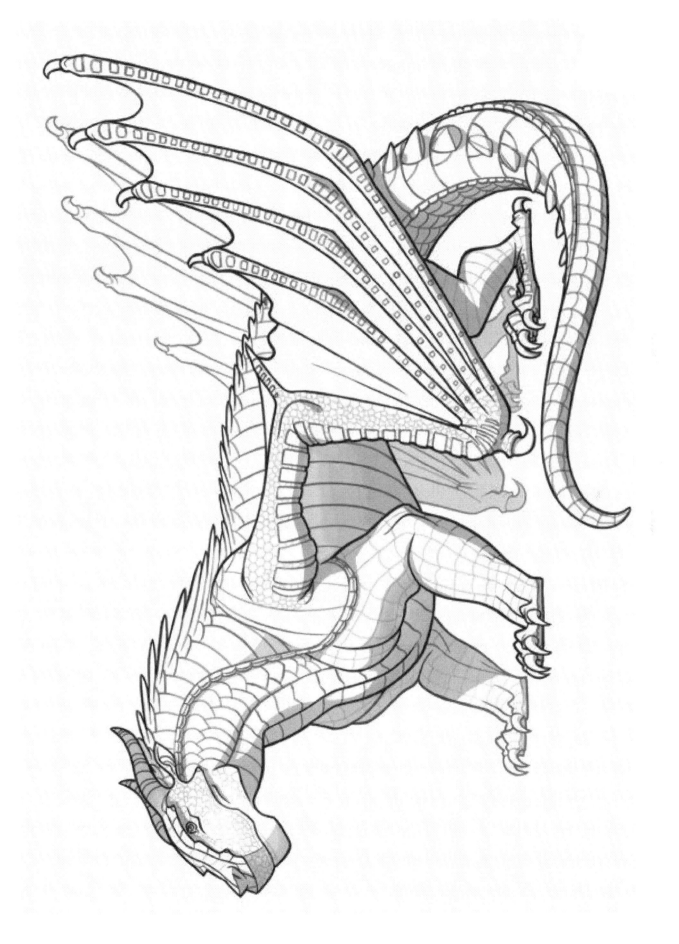

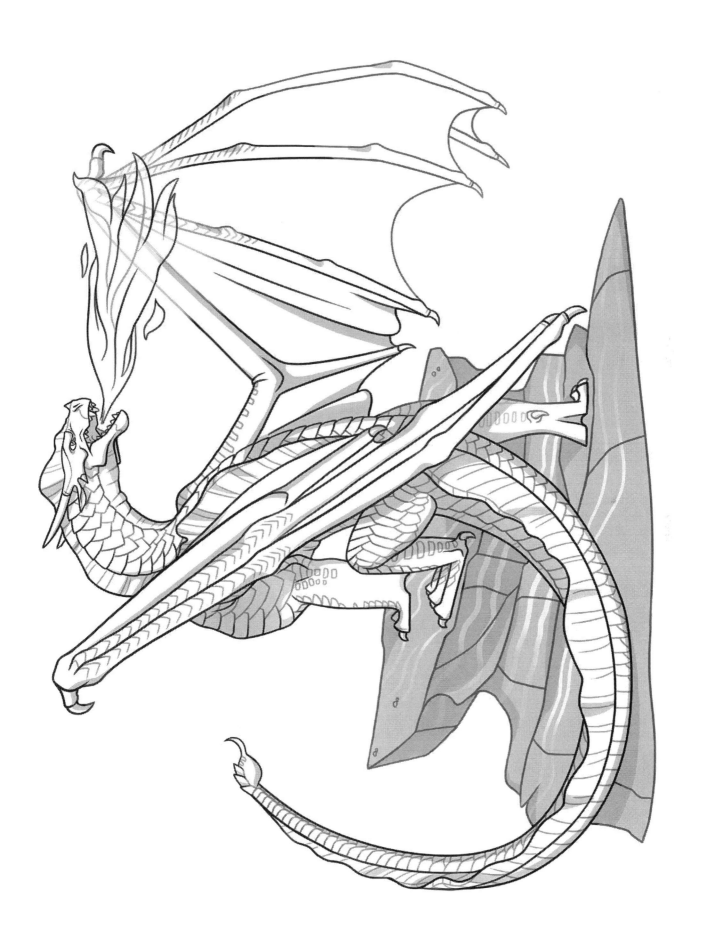

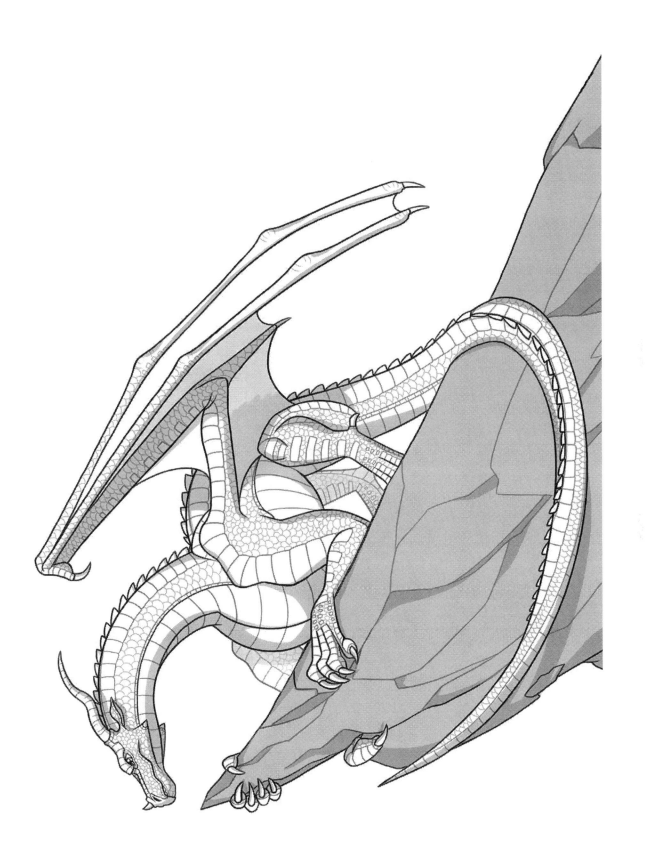

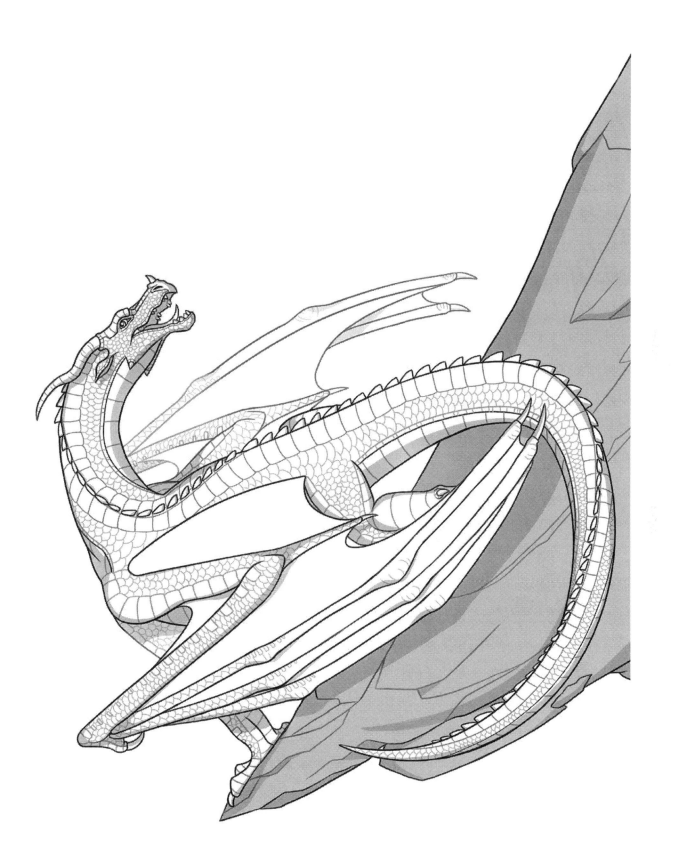

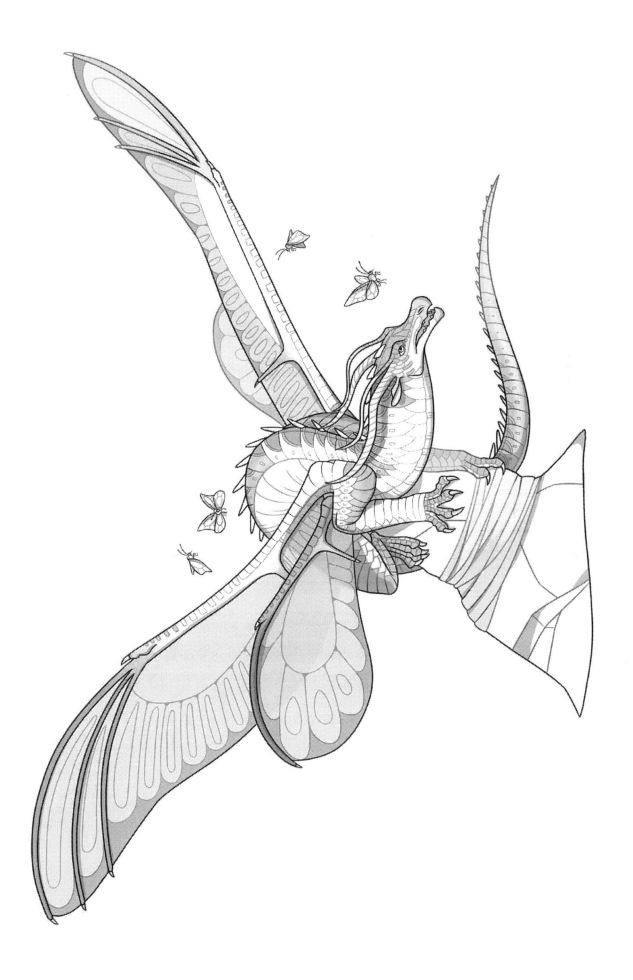

Dear Customer

A thousand thanks for purchasing this book. We really apreciate
We are a small family company and thanks to you, we exist.

We are young but we have big hearts and a big vision
We do our best to offer the HIGHEST QUALITY books for you to enjoy.
If you enjoy this book, we have a very modest request: please take a few seconds to leave us a review on this book's Amazon product page.

You can't imagine how pleased we are for the support, and we are doing our best to deliver you the best books.
We wish you only the best, and if you want to reach us for inquiries please send an email at:
nikolas.norbert@yahoo.com

Sincerely

Nikolas Norbert

Made in United States
Troutdale, OR
01/13/2024

16894307R00053